The Art Contest, No Cheating Allowed

By Steven Banks
Illustrated by Robert Dress

The Bikini Bottom Art Society was having an art contest, and first prize was a membership to their fancy club.

"If I could be in that club, maybe working at the Krusty Krab won't seem as hopeless," Squidward said, sighing.

Squidward went to the Art Society building to enter the contest. There he saw Squilliam Fancyson, his old rival.

"Good luck, Squidward. You'll need it! I've seen your paintings . . . and I'm one of the judges!" said Squilliam.

"I've got to paint the greatest painting of my life!" said Squidward.
He painted seventeen paintings, but they were all awful!
"I'll never win the contest with these!" he said, moaning.

Squidward heard SpongeBob humming outside, so he leaned out his window.

"Hey!" he shouted. "Keep it down! I'm trying to paint!"

"Sorry, Squidward," said SpongeBob. "I'm just drawing some pictures in the sand."

Squidward couldn't believe his eyes. SpongeBob's sand pictures were amazing!

"Uh, hello there, SpongeBob," said Squidward. "How about you paint a picture for me sometime . . . like today!"

"Really?" asked an excited SpongeBob.

"Sure," replied Squidward. "I have a big hole in one of my walls, and I could cover it up with one of your paintings."

"By the way, you're not entering the Bikini Bottom Art Society contest, are you?" asked Squidward as they walked toward SpongeBob's house.

"What contest?" asked SpongeBob.

"Nothing! Never mind!" said Squidward.

"Gary!" said SpongeBob. "I get to do a painting for Squidward! Isn't that great?"

"Meow," said Gary.

SpongeBob got ready to paint. "I sure hope I can paint something that Squidward likes enough to cover up the hole in his wall!"

SpongeBob painted all night. The next morning Squidward came to pick out a painting.

"Will any of these do?" asked an exhausted SpongeBob.

"I guess I could use this one," said Squidward, choosing a painting. "This will definitely win me first place, uh, I mean, this will definitely cover up the hole on my wall!" Squidward grabbed the painting and hurried home.

"Hmmm, now I'll just put my name on the painting, and everyone will think I did it." Squidward clapped his tentacles together. "I can't wait to see the look on Squilliam's face when he hands first prize to me!"

Squidward showed SpongeBob's painting to Squilliam and the other judges.

"This can't be your painting," cried Squilliam. "It's too good!"

"I know," replied Squidward.

"I never thought I'd say this, but first prize goes to Squidward Tentacles," said Squilliam, handing Squidward a Bikini Bottom Art Society membership card.

Just then SpongeBob came into the room. "Hey, Squidward!" he said. "I saw a flyer for this art contest and I thought I'd check it out. Did you know there was a contest today?"

"Uh, no, I didn't," said Squidward, trying to hide SpongeBob's painting.

"Huh, that painting behind you looks just like the painting I did," said SpongeBob.

Squidward shook his head. "No! It's not. It's a completely different painting!"

"Awww, Squidward! You entered my painting into the contest, how sweet!" said SpongeBob.

"Is this true, Squidward?" a hopeful Squilliam asked.

"But why did you paint your initials over mine?" asked SpongeBob, confused.

Squilliam took a wet cloth to the painting and erased Squidward's initials to reveal SpongeBob's initials underneath it.

"I knew it!" Squilliam squealed. "I knew Squidward couldn't paint anything that good!"

He took away Squidward's membership card and tore it up.

"I'm sorry!" cried Squidward. "I just wanted to be in your club so badly!"

Squidward turned to Spongebob. "I'm sorry I tried to pass off your painting as my own."

"That's okay, Squidward. I forgive you," said SpongeBob.

Squilliam held up one of his own paintings. "You have to paint like *me* if you want to be in this club, Squidward!" he said.

Just then a young man walked in. "Uh, Mr. Fancyson, sir," said the man, interrupting. "I just finished painting that other painting for you. You weren't at home, so I decided to drop it off here. Hope that's okay," he said.

"What!? You don't paint your own paintings, either!" exclaimed Squidward.

Squilliam gulped. "Uh . . . I . . . just remembered . . . I have to go somewhere!" He ran away as fast as he could.

"I have a confession to make," said one of the other judges. "I don't paint my paintings either. In fact I found the one that got me into the club in a garbage can," he admitted.

"My mother painted mine," confessed a contestant.

Finally the truth came out.

Not one of the judges or contestants had painted a single painting!

"It looks like no one can belong to the Bikini Bottom Art Society except for SpongeBob SquarePants," said Squidward.

"But I don't want to be the only person in the club," said SpongeBob. "I have an idea! Let's start a new club that everyone can be in! But what should it be?"

Everyone was silent while SpongeBob tried to come up with a new club.

"I know!" he suddenly cried. "We'll call it the Bikini Bottom Bubble Blowing Society!"

And that's what they did!